For Anne

This 1988 edition published by Derrydale Books,
distributed by Crown Publishers, Inc.
225 Park Avenue South, New York,
New York 10003.

ISBN - 0 - 517 - 66273 - 6

h g f e d c b a

Library of Congress Cataloging-in-Publication Data
Dalmais, Anne-Marie, 1954.
Best bedtime stories of Mother Bear / by Anne Marie Dalmais.
p. 32 cm. 19,5 x 25,5
Summary : Presents two stories within a story, as Mother Bear
relates bedtime tales to soothe her cubs to sleep.
ISBN 0-517-66273-6
1. Children's stories, French-Translations into English.
2. Children's stories, English-Translations from French.
(1. Bears-Fiction. 2. Short stories) I. Title.
PZ7.D166Be 1988 - (E)-dc 19 - 88-10862 CIP AC

THE BEST BEDTIME STORIES

OF MOTHER BEAR

Stories by Anne-Marie Dalmais
illustrated by Violayne Hulné

English translation by DIANE COHEN

DERRYDALE BOOKS
New York

"What's this, my little rascal, you haven't finished your bath yet?!" Mother Bear scolds her cubs in her deep, stern voice. "I thought I'd find you in your pajamas and nightgown. You've been splashing about in this tub for at least half an hour. That's enough!" These two little bears, brother and sister, have been happily paddling away in a great big wooden barrel in front of the fireplace where the heat from the fire keeps the water warm. The warm water feels wonderful! The cubs sing a duet that they made up all by themselves.

Bubbles, tiny bubbles, who wants my pretty bubbles?
Drip, drop, drip, won't you join us for a dip?!

"If you don't get out this instant, I'm leaving without telling my stories!" Mother Bear threatens.

"Oh no, Mother!" her little girl cries. "I'll get dressed right away. Please, pretty please, tell me a story!"

"And Mother, I'm going to clean up all this mess!" says her little boy. "Please, pretty please, tell us two stories!"

Of course, it takes some time to keep these promises. First our bathers must dry themselves, rubbing their thick fur over and over again so it shines like silk. Then they must dig out their pajamas from the middle of the terrible clutter. And then they must put the room back in order.

Mother Bear congratulates them saying, "Bravo, charming children!" and announces, "Since it's snowing and it's very cold outside, I'm going to tell you summertime stories!"

The Adventurers
at the Far End of the Garden

Once upon a time there was a sweet little cub named Tootie. Why this name, you ask? You shall soon see...

This little cub had arrived at his grandmother's house where he was spending his vacation with his friend Dizzy the dog. Grandma Moonlight gave them both a big kiss.

Oh, it's wonderful, once again, to visit the little wooden house that is so cheerful and homey. It is so much fun to play in the huge garden at the edge of the forest. There is much to discover at Grandma's house and in her garden.

Sometimes Tootie and Dizzy played till they were out of breath, running, jumping, going around and around the garden. At other times they told each other stories, stretched out on the grass among the flowers, watching the clouds float by.

The garden is a marvelous place. They wished they could stay in it forever!

"Maybe we could sleep outside tonight," Tootie proposed.

"Oh! Yes, yes! Great idea!" Dizzy agreed.

When they asked Grandma Moonlight she gladly gave her permission.

"But you won't be the least bit afraid?" she asked, smiling.

"Oh, no! Of course not!" Tootie exclaimed, very sure of himself. That very afternoon, the two friends set up a tent very very far away from the house. They pretended they were at the end of the world.

After a festive dinner topped off by a delicious apple pie, served with vanilla ice cream so it tasted especially yummy, our great adventurers, Tootie and Dizzy, headed toward the far end of the garden to their solitary campsite.

"Tralala, tralala!" Tootie hummed. "Our vacation is starting out great!"

"Yes, yes, yes! Great, great, great!" Dizzy echoed.

They remained for a few minutes in front of their tent quietly watching the vast sky darken in the twilight. Grandma Moonlight came to wish them good night. Since she was a good and attentive grandmother, she brought them a flashlight. "It could always come in handy," she said. She also brought two extra pillows, saying, "you'll be more comfortable." "Sleep well, sweet dreams," she added, as she left them.

Tootie and Dizzy glided under their tents and carefully shut themselves in.

"It's a real little house!" the cub marveled.

"We're perfectly safe and sound!" added the dog, gratefully.

"And now, let's go to bed!" Tootie yelled.

"To bed, to bed, the first one in bed wins! Hey, that's me!" declared Dizzy, who, in the wink of an eye, slipped into his sleeping bag.

"This is so comfy," the cub said, curling up, nice and cozy under his quilted cover.

"Oh, yes! I think I'm going to sleep very well!" the dog exclaimed with a loud yawn.

But suddenly, a gust of wind bent the branches of the big pine tree just above the tent. They creaked frightfully. The two friends, terrified, sat up at once with teeth chattering.

"We... we can't stay here..." Tootie stammered.

"No, it doesn't look good," Dizzy admitted.

In a flash, they pulled up the campsite and ran toward the house with all their stuff. They stumbled over roots, almost falling several times. How quickly the garden had changed. The eerie shadows and strange whispers made it seem unfriendly and unsettling.

Still, our adventurers didn't want to go inside the house. They were embarrassed. So, feeling their way in the dim light of their flashlight, they managed, to set up their tent on the lawn, just in front of the porch. They felt better near the house.

But they didn't take the time to drive in all the pegs so the tent was crooked. Since they were in such a hurry to take shelter inside, they didn't care. But then the weather vane started to make a scary sound...

This was more than our friends could stand and they took off as fast as their little paws would go!

Shaking like leaves, as pale as ghosts, Tootie and Dizzy forgot
their pride and dashed full speed ahead into the house! They were
so relieved when they closed the heavy wooden door behind them!

"We're still not going to sleep in our rooms!" declared Tootie,
who, barely having put one paw in the entrance hall, had regained
all his self-confidence. "Let's camp out in the living room!" So they
put up their tent between two chairs and dived into their sleeping
bags.

This time "the adventurers at the far end of the garden" really did fall asleep! Grandma Moonlight, who had heard the commotion, went downstairs and found, in the middle of her living room, the two explorers in their new campsite. She smiled gently. "I expected as much. They were scared out there in the wide open spaces. Tootie is a real cutie, but sometimes he brags a little. He likes to toot his own horn, that's all. It's nothing serious, he'll grow out of it. As for his friend, Dizzy, he's very nice too, but just a wee little silly. They're a good pair after all, young, but lots of fun.

Their kind grandmother lingered a few moments to watch them thinking. They're so sweet when they're asleep. She looked forward to spending the summer with this pair. "What fun we're going to have..."

Hiking Near The Clouds!

Once upon a time there was a friendly and very happy family of bears. The Father, HoneyComb, loved to go on long walks and outings. He was a very energetic bear! And no one could make better jams and jellies than Blackberry, the mother. Their little cub, Cookie charmed everyone around her with her sweet disposition and gracious smile.

During the summer, our three bears stayed in the mountains, in a small, cozy lodge surrounded by greenery.

One afternoon, while the family was sitting on a wooden bench out on the terrace enjoying the sun, HoneyComb announced that the next day he was going hiking with their young cousin Billy Goat. He unfolded a big map to show the trail he planned to follow. "I want to come with you!" the little cub cried. "It would be much too difficult," her mother objected.

But Cookie begged and pleaded and flashed her adorable smile, so her parents finally gave her permission to join them. Before going to bed, she set her alarm so that the next morning she would wake up early.

When the alarm clock rang bright and early the next day,

Cookie yawned, rubbed her eyes, and jumped out of bed. She mustn't keep her father waiting! Quickly she slipped into her clothes — a comfortable little dress and a very warm jacket.

Then she prepared her backpack. She packed a sweater, a woolen scarf, her pocketknife, two handkerchiefs, a rubber ball, and a notebook.

Next she strapped on her canteen and said good-bye to her mother.

"Have a good time, my little Cookie and be careful!" advised Blackberry.

"Yes, yes," the cub promised and gave her mother a big kiss. "See you tomorrow!"

20

At first the walk was delightful. The trio crossed sunny meadows sprinkled with wild flowers. The little cub had never seen such pretty colors!

"Oh! What beautiful flowers!

"Hooray, hooray for the mountains!" she exclaimed, clapping her paws together.

A little higher up she was surprised by the sight and sounds of bubbling mountain streams that tumbled down the slopes, jumped over the tops of the rocks, cascaded down again. The mountaineers' clear and spirited singing added to the harmonious sounds.

Cookie felt she could go on and on listening to these beautiful songs.

And every time she became thirsty, she stopped to drink, cupping her paw to get a mouthful of the sparkling clean water. Or for fun she filled her canteen in the current.

But gradually the trail grew narrower and narrower, steeper and steeper. It became difficult to walk since the meadow's soft grass was replaced by sharp pebbles that hurt their paws and by big, clumsy stones.

The peaceful walk turned into a perilous climb.

It was so hard to keep going! Out of breath, Cookie huffed and puffed. She slowed down! She sighed. She was hot. She didn't want to complain, but this steep trail wasn't any fun at all! It climbed straight up! What was worse it became a ledge, hanging over the valley far below! And there was no railing to hold. HoneyComb didn't seem the least bit worried. And Cookie's crazy cousin Billy Goat didn't think twice about going over to the edge to exclaim, "Wow! look at the beautiful view!"

When she saw the house down in the valley looking as small as toys, and noticed, next to her, a tremendous gaping space, Cookie suddenly became very dizzy. Instead of admiring the countryside, she started to cry.

"I don't want to keep going... I'm scared..." She sobbed. She hiccupped. She trembled.

Her kind father tried to cheer her up as best as he could. First he pulled a bar of chocolate out of his spacious backpack and immediately gave her a big piece.

Then he called her by many sweet names that made her laugh, despite her worries.

"My precious pine-cone, my fragrant wild strawberry, my cute little clover flower, my scrumptious triple-scoop ice cream cone, my funny pineapple upside-down cake, my beautiful shooting star...

These silly endearments, together with the delicious taste of the chocolate comforted the little cub. She took a deep breath and raised her head.

Seeing that his Cookie had calmed down, HoneyComb quietly explained to her that to avoid getting dizzy she should not look down into the valley, and she should always look toward the clouds or the mountain peak.

So Cookie continued her hike, in between Billy Goat, who stepped aside to make room for her, and her father, who looked after and guided her.

The sun had set in the sky when our mountaineers finally reached the lodge where they were going to sleep.

"Yippee!" Cookie yelled, pushing open the wooden door that creaked in welcome.

After her dizzy climb and at the very end of this long hike, it was a relief to find a real little house at the very top of this mountain. While her father prepared dinner, Cookie went to pick some white flowers.

The little cub had never been so hungry for her supper. The hike and all the excitement had given her quite an appetite! Her eyes sparkled, she relished the soup, bread and butter, honey cakes and jam rolls. Then, one last climb she hoisted herself up onto her wooden bunk and fell asleep almost instantly, with a big, happy smile on her sweet face. She hardly had the time to notice, through the window of the lodge, the brilliant stars of this unforgettable summer night...

As they followed, the fearless Cookie step by step along her dangerous ascent, the two cubs, brother and sister, began to feel tired themselves, as if they, too, had walked, hiked, and climbed up the mountain. They closed their eyes to hear the end of the story. But their heads began to roll gently to the right and to the left...

Overcome by drowsiness, our cubs soon slid onto their cushions and fell asleep, curled up into balls near their mother's chair. Kind Mother Bear then carried her two dozing bundles of joy, one by one, to their beds...